A BOOK OF FRUIT

by Barbara Hirsch Lember

Ticknor & Fields Books for Young Readers

New York · 1994

For my daughters, Jessica and Amanda

ACKNOWLEDGMENTS: For their generous help providing crop information and the opportunity to photograph their fruit, I wish to thank the following growers: Dr. Barbara Muse, Scott Robertello, and David Guy of Delaware Valley College; Solly Brothers; Pan American Groves; Elson's Exotics; and Haines & Haines. Special thanks to Lynne Rubin of Victoriannie; Helene Pasternak; Tracy Buehrer at Indian Rock Produce; and Dr. Stephen K-M. Tim, Brooklyn Botanic Garden. Thanks, too, to my family and friends for their consistent interest, support, and assistance; to Norma Jean Sawicki for giving me the opportunity to create this book, and to David Saylor for his wonderful artistic sensibility—it has been a pleasure to work with them.

NOTE: The photograph on the last page shows a lime grove.

Published by Ticknor & Fields Books for Young Readers, A Houghton Mifflin company, 215 Park Avenue South, New York, New York 10003. Copyright © 1994 by Barbara Hirsch Lember. All rights reserved. For information about permission to reproduce selections from this book, write to Permissions, Ticknor & Fields, 215 Park Avenue South, New York, New York 10003. Manufactured in the United States of America. Book design by David Saylor. The text of this book is set in 36 point ITC Giovanni Book. The photographs were taken with black-and-white infrared film and hand-tinted; they are reproduced in full color.   HOR 10 9 8 7 6 5 4 3 2 1

LIBRARY OF CONGRESS CATALOGING-IN-PUBLICATION DATA: Lember, Barbara Hirsch. A book of fruit / by Barbara Hirsch Lember. p. cm. ISBN 0-395-66989-8 1. Fruit—Juvenile literature. [1. Fruit.] I. Title. SB357.2.L45 1994 634—dc20 94-4067 CIP AC

Fruit ...

Peach

Peach orchard

Strawberries

Strawberry field

Orange

Orange grove

Bananas

Banana plantation

Cherries

Cherry orchard

Raspberries

Raspberry field

Grapes

Grape vineyard

Watermelon

Watermelon field

Starfruits

Starfruit grove

Blueberries

Blueberry field

Pear

Pear orchard

Cranberries

Cranberry bog

Tomato

Tomato field

Apple

Apple orchard

Fruit grows in many places.